Dear Parent:

In this charming story, Emily Elizabeth learns a lesson
that many of us take a lifetime to acquire: We can count our
true friends on the fingers of one hand. A true friend is
someone who believes in you and stands by you—no matter
what. A true friend doesn't waver when less loyal buddies
succumb to the social pressure of turning away. It's easy to be
a fair-weather friend, but challenging to be a true and loyal
one. And it's as important to *be* one as it is to have one. In
The Doggy Detectives, Clifford and T-Bone stand up to the
doubters and prove to be Emily Elizabeth's loyal friends.

Young children face similar challenges to their loyalties. When,
for example, the members of a self-appointed "in" crowd of
preschoolers or primary graders decide not to play with some
hapless child, and urge others to join them, friendships are
severely tested. Sometimes a child is forced to choose between
two friends. "I won't play with you anymore if you play with
him," is an all-too-common threat. You might expect your
child to rise to the occasion and say, "If you want to play with
me, you have to include **X** because both of you are my
friends." Don't be disappointed, however, if this doesn't
happen. It takes time to feel socially confident enough to take
this stand. Even adults waffle in similar situations, and many
regretfully recall such scenes from childhood.

When your child is confronted with such a challenge, sharing
stories of similar situations can be very helpful—provided you
don't portray yourself as having been conflict-free and noble
at all times. Let your child know
you've been there, understand the
struggle, and provide some
prudent guidance.

Adele M. Brodkin, Ph.D.

Visit Clifford at scholastic.com/clifford

ISBN 0-439-22462-4

Library of Congress Cataloging-in-Publication Data is available

10 9 8 7 6 5 4 3 2 1   01 02 03 04 05 06

Printed in the U.S.A.   24
First printing, June 2001

Clifford THE BIG RED DOG®
The Doggy Detectives

Adapted by David L. Harrison

Illustrated by José Maria Cardona

**Based on the Scholastic book series
"Clifford The Big Red Dog"
by Norman Bridwell**

From the television script
"To Catch a Bird" by Meg McLaughlin

Cartwheel
·B·O·O·K·S·®

SCHOLASTIC INC.
New York   Toronto   London   Auckland   Sydney   Mexico City
New Delhi   Hong Kong

When Jetta won the spelling bee,
She bragged and bragged to Emily.
"My medal is a gorgeous sight!
Watch it glisten in the light!

Emily, hide my spelling prize

While I play soccer with the guys.

I'm trusting you to hide my gold

In case some thief is feeling bold."

A crow as crafty as could be
Was watching Jetta from a tree.
"I'm so sly she'll never know
Who stole her medal," said the crow.

He chuckled with a greedy caw,
Flew so fast that no one saw,
Stole the gold without a sound,
And no one knew he'd been around.

When Jetta put her sweater on,
She cried, "Oh, no! My medal's gone!
Who took it, Mac? Do you know who?
I bet I know! And you do, too!"

I have news to tell you guys!
Jetta lost her golden prize!
She won it at the spelling bee,
And guess who stole it—Emily!

"Emily Elizabeth, give it back!

I know you took it! So does Mac!

You're jealous just because I won!

What a terrible thing you've done!"

"Jetta, I would never steal!

You don't know how bad I feel!

Perhaps you lost it coming here.

Perhaps your medal's very near."

Above them laughed the crafty crow,

"Just how near, you'll never know!"

"We know Emily's not to blame!
It's up to us to clear her name!"

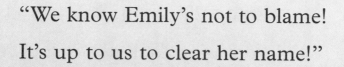

"How do we prove it?
What do we use?"

"Detectives always look for clues.

We'll start by sniffing around the park."

"And if we find a clue,
We'll bark!"

"That thief had better watch his tail
Now that we are on his trail!
This feather makes me sneeze, *AH-CHOO!*"

"T-Bone, try to find a clue!"

"A shiny mirror!" said the crow.

"I'll steal this, too, before they know.

I'll add this mirror to my gold.

Shiny mirrors make me bold!"

"Emily, what is wrong with you?
Now you took my mirror, too!"

"Jetta, why do you think I'd lie?
I feel so bad that I could cry!"

"Emily did it again!" said Mac.

"She won't give Jetta's mirror back."

"She didn't take it!" Clifford howled.

Mac just looked at him and scowled.

"Clifford, what if she really hid
The gold and mirror? Maybe she did!"

"She didn't!" Clifford said with a shout.
"Now hurry! Time is running out!"

"I just hope we're not too late.
We'll use your shiny bow for bait.
And when we catch the thief, you'll see
You're wrong to blame my Emily!"

"Clifford! Look! See what I meant?
Your Emily is not innocent!
She's going to steal my shiny bow!
Admit it, Clifford. Now we know."

"Cleo, dear, you've lost your bow.

Let me help before I go.

Poor Jetta needs me with her now.

We've got to find her things somehow."

The crow appeared but no one saw.

And no one heard his greedy caw.

He stole the bow and no one knew,

But this time T-Bone found the clue.

"My bow is missing!"
Cleo howled.
"She took it after all!"
she scowled.

"She didn't take it!"
Clifford sighed.

"I found a feather!"
T-Bone cried.

Look up there! You see that crow?

We've seen that crow before, you know.

We've found his feathers very near

To where Jetta's things would disappear!

Cleo! T-Bone! Here's our crook!
His nest is full of what he took!
I've never seen such shiny loot!
Jetta's things, and more to boot!
CLIFFORD

"Jetta, are you satisfied?

Now you know I never lied."

"I was wrong, I realize!

Forgive me! I apologize!"

Mac and Cleo,
What about you?

Whimper! Whine!
We're sorry, too!